His Peace
Her Poison

Christina Louise

His Peace
Her Poison

Christina Louise

Pen2Pad Ink
Publishing

Library of Congress Cataloging–In–Publication Data

Name: Worth, Christina, author.
Title: His Peace Her Poison/
Christina Worth

ISBN: 978-1-970135-78-7 Paperback

Published in the United States by
Pen2Pad Ink Publishing.
www.pen2padink.org

Requests to publish work from this book or to contact the author should be sent to:

Christina Louise retains the rights to all images.

His Peace, Her Poison

"Why are you being short with me?" He asked.

"I'm not sure what you are expecting from me, Donovan..." I answered.

"Well...yeah but..."

"I am not your safety net, D. Don't misunderstand. I forgave you, but I will never forget what you said. People have this crazy idea that words mean nothing. They mean something. And from you... they meant everything. I appreciate the journey, but this is where I get off the ride. I pray you find what you are looking for."

Click. The END button on my phone gave me the confirmation I needed. Every pain. Every single ounce of anguish and despair from this 14-year friendship was over. I finally had the vaccine for the venom that was in me for so long.

His Peace, Her Poison

Chapter 1

Basketball is life. I took that to heart when I was in middle school to avoid bothering my mother with a more expensive habit like band or cheerleading. Anytime you saw me, I had a basketball, *And 1* shorts, and the one pair of Jordan's my mom could afford for the year. I appreciated them though. My mom worked hard to put all five of us through school on her own. She wasn't going to let her role as a single parent keep us from making it in life. Seeing her work hard gave me the will to do the same. Whatever I did. Whoever I cared for. I did it wholeheartedly.

Basketball also kept me sane in my hometown of Precious, Mississippi. If you could picture a small town, cut it in half and you would have my town. Stoplights? We only had one. Fast food restaurants? Please. You better head over to Aunt Pearl's Snack Shack that extended from the left side of her house like an extra arm. Only in my town could a tractor, horse, and F150 be on the road at the same time and cause a traffic jam. I always knew my heart and dreams were bigger than where I lived.

The only time I really had the chance to venture outside of Precious was on basketball field trips. We played some of the other small towns in the area. Precious High School was so small that Kindergarten to 12th grade was all in the same building. I was happy to always be on a bus leaving Precious because I also had the chance to hang out with my best friend Monica. I wasn't a big talker, but Monica did enough talking for the both of us. I didn't mind her wagging tongue, and she didn't mind my many imitations of a mime due to my shyness. However, Monica's mouth could sometimes put me in some awkward situations. One of those times was at a basketball tournament when I was in eighth grade.

When I was not thinking about basketball or my grades, I will admit that I thought about boys. Basketball tournaments always gave me the chance to see cute boys. I wouldn't talk to them, but I would do what most girls my age did: giggle in a big group, point, and try to act like I wasn't talking about them. When we would walk around, we would end up outside the gym by the concession stand talking and looking. This tournament, however, was different. Yes, there were cute guys. But...there was one. He was 5 foot 10, skin dipped in caramel, athletically built with gentle brown eyes. I watched his mouth move as he talked to some of his teammates across from where I was with Monica and my other team members.

"Lani," Monica started, "You ok?"

I couldn't stop staring at him. It was almost like he glowed while standing there. I was in love.

"Lani!" Monica nudged me. I shook my head and looked at her.

"What?" I asked. She followed my eyes and started smiling.

"Oh...I see. Go talk to him!" Monica insisted.

"Really, Mon? You know that's not going to happen." I answered.

"Oh yes it will." Monica left our group. I tried to get her before she moved, but she moved too fast! All the other girls followed while I stayed toward the back and hopefully out of sight.

"Uh...excuse me," Monica started, "What's your name?" She asked the caramel adonis. All the guys looked around and snickered while he stood there shocked.

"Uh...Donovan." He said slowly.

"Well, Donovan, my best friend thinks you are cute. There she is over there. Her name is Lalani."

I froze. The only part of me that could move was my eyes as I looked on the ground and around trying not to appear so obvious. When the feeling finally came back to my legs, I walked away really fast and went back to sit in the stands. I could hear the dudes laughing as I walked away, but I was too embarrassed to care. I sat down on the bleacher and breathed.

Inhaled. Exhaled. I tried to pay attention to the game on the court, but my mind was swirling. I loved Monica, but sometimes I wanted to choke her.

"Why did you run?!" Monica asked.

"Why you think! You know I wasn't ready for that! Plus, he has a girlfriend. I saw them together earlier." I answered.

"Oh. Oops." Monica said, shrugging her shoulders. I put my head in my lap and tried to catch my breath. I stayed in the bleachers in that same spot the rest of that day. Eventually, it was time for us to leave the tournament. I was walking down the stairs of the bleachers looking down to make sure I didn't miss a step when a large body bumped into me.

"I'm sorry I--"

"My bad. Lalani, right?" There he was. Looking at me. I did my best to play it cool.

"Yeah...Yeah...um...that's me. Listen, I'm sorry about earlier. I don't have control over my friend's mouth. And I'm not trying to start anything between you and your girlfriend. "

"It's ok. We all have someone like that around us. I appreciate you for that. Good game earlier." *Wait... he watched my game?!*

"Thanks. I better go before my bus leaves me."

"True. You have a good night."

"You too." I floated down the rest of those steps that night and smiled all the way home on the bus.

Christina Louise

Chapter 2

I made the "big" move from middle school to high school at Precious. My building didn't change, but I did. I started to fill out in different places, and basketball shorts were no longer my norm. My chocolate skin shined with lotion. My butt finally made an appearance, but I was still skinny everywhere else and a founding member of the itty-bitty titty committee.

While everyone else was giving up their goodies more than Ciara dancing, I was a virgin and perfectly fine with it. I wanted my first time to be memorable and with someone I could share a lifetime. I wasn't going to find that in Precious. If everyone didn't know everyone, you were probably kin to them. Yeah...I'll pass. Plus, my mind and heart were still with Donovan. We saw each other at different tournaments our schools competed in. Both of our teams even went to state championships for basketball. When he was around, everything and everyone disappeared. I loved when that happened.

I graduated from high school with a 3.8 GPA and a dream to attend Spelman College. My mother was NOT having that. After my dad left, she had big problems with any of us leaving to go far from home. Against my better judgment, I stayed close to home for college. I tried to make the best of it, my heart was in Atlanta no matter how much I tried to make things better.

One of the few highlights of my college experience was hearing about Donovan. Monica went to the same college as him which is about 5 hours away from mine. I never missed an opportunity to see how he was doing or to have Monica tell him hello. Monica was convinced he looked like a goat, but he was a cute goat in my eyes. Despite how she felt about his appearance, she would always keep me updated on what he was doing. If only that feeling would spread over my entire college experience.

It didn't. By the end of my sophomore

year, I was a wreck mentally and emotionally. I was three hours from home. My mama didn't come to visit. And... I was broke. I started braiding and found a job that I could carpool to. When I needed somewhere to stay, Victoria made sure I had a roof over my head. I stayed with her as long as I could, but I still wanted my own. It wasn't because Victoria's dad was a drug addict. It wasn't because I didn't love Victoria. I just needed somewhere where I could think: A place where I wasn't doing more for others or for survival.

I was struggling mentally, emotionally, and socially. I longed for a relationship with my mother since I gave up what I wanted for her. I wanted someone to help me relieve some of the pressure that came with feeling so alone. I craved some type of happiness that I couldn't find in myself.

Chapter 3

When you are alone by choice, you do not mind spending time alone. You don't hate people, but you can live without them for a while. But when alone is by force, you look for anyone or anything to relieve you of that pain. Tobias was my relief. He came in like Superman saving me from the villainous loneliness that I could not handle alone. When I needed help, Tobias was there. I had no problems moving to Louisiana in order to be with him. He was my comfort blanket, and I accepted that in the place of what I could not have at the time: Donovan. The comfort we felt with each other led to us taking our relationship to an intimate level. He wasn't my knight in shining armor, but he was present. Present worked for me. His presence also led to an even bigger present I found out in the bathroom of my job.

"Can we talk?" I asked. We were sitting at home after I came home from work.

"Sure. What's up?" Tobias asked.

"Well...uh...I am pregnant."

"Oh." He looked around the apartment and nodded his head slowly.

"Ummm...anything else besides 'oh'?" I asked.

"Well...do you want to keep it or do you want to...you know..."

"Get rid of it?"

"Yeah."

"Tobias, you knew our choice to have sex could possibly lead to this. Don't act like I was in the bed alone. I'm not the Virgin Mary."

"Ok!," He said with his hands raised,

"We havin' the baby. I guess we need to get married, huh?"

My eyes widened. "Do what now?"

"Well you havin' my baby. It's only right."

"Uh...no. I'm not marrying you because I'm pregnant. We'll see where this goes with the pregnancy, but I'm not about that unhappy marriage life."

We stayed together a couple of months, but we eventually decided to go our separate ways. Tobias could not deal with the idea of having children. Eight months after his unnecessary proposal, I gave birth to my two favorite jewels in the world: Josiah Macon and Lola Angelia Jones. When I saw them in the delivery, something clicked. My pity party had to come to an end. They had to see a better side of me. A side that believed in herself. A side that didn't let my situation keep me from progress. I put my big girl drawers on and vowed to be better for them and myself.

When the twins were at the age for daycare, I went into straight hustler mode. You would have thought I woke up listening to Rick Ross and Beyoncé every morning. I woke at 4 AM every morning, dropped the twins at daycare, went to class, and then went to work. After work, I picked up twins and brought them home to our one-bedroom apartment in the projects. The twins went to sleep, I finished homework, and went to sleep around 11 PM or Midnight. The next day, I woke up at 4 AM and did it again.

Four and half years later, I walked across the stage of Southeastern Louisiana University. The announcement of my name led to eruptions of screams from Mrs. Linda, the daycare lady, and my family. I ended up in tears by the time I finished crossing the stage. No, things didn't start the way they should have. I could have given up after having twins. I was a single parent on Medicaid and food stamps, but I was a college graduate. And I was ready for bigger and better.

Chapter 4

Miami, Florida. Sunrays. Beautiful ocean views. And...Me? I knew Miami was my choice, but how could I afford it? I had children, and I had no intentions of keeping them in projects and food stamp dependency places. Fortunately, help came from an unexpected place.

"They can come stay with me." My mother said. I froze with the phone in my hand. Is she...did she say...wait...is this the same woman?

"Wait, you said they can stay with...you...like in your house?

With you?" I asked in disbelief.

"Yes, child, with me. At least until you get on your feet." I thought about it. While I may not have the best relationship with her, it doesn't mean my children do not have to.

"Ok. But I will come get them as soon as I get everything together." I brought the kids to her, gave them the biggest hugs I could, and set my sights for Miami. It was my choice and a breath of fresh air.

I found a "pay the bills" job and an apartment that the twins and I could live in comfortably. Since I was no longer multi-tasking with a job, kids, and school, I actually had time to create a Facebook page. I was scrolling one day and saw a face I knew very well: Donovan Mitchell. He still had the same smile. His face aged beautifully. I clicked on his profile and saw different pictures of him. He was taller. He still had the same athletic body, but it was broader and more defined. His skin still looked like someone sun kissed a brown Crayola color and shaded him in. He had graduated a couple of years before me from Jackson State and started working at a firm in Miami. Wait...
MIAMI? Shut up!

I clicked "Add as A Friend" and sat back in my chair. Well...it's a small world after all. (Did you start singing it? Don't feel bad. I did too.) Whatever God was doing, I was here for it.

Donovan's presence in Miami was great, but I missed two little people more: my babies! It took about 6 months, but Lola and Josiah finally moved to Miami with me and settled into their life with Mommy. During this time, Donovan accepted my friend request. We messaged each other to see how the other was doing or to talk about kids (Donovan had a daughter with his high school sweetheart.). Messaging eventually turned into face-to-face conversations. I would meet him at his house or at a restaurant. He never came to my house. Beautiful or not, I was very protective of my babies.

I was okay with our friendship, but I will admit I was hoping for more. However, I didn't know how he felt about it. So, I waited for him to make the first move. I felt like we were moving to another level until a Facebook post put that thought in limbo. We were having our usual conversation at Matches during happy hour before I had to pick up the twins.

"So I see I'm not the only female companion you have." I stated.

"What are you talking about?" He asked. I showed him a picture of the post I was referring to. It was a picture of him with some girl. The caption for the post stated "BAE for life".

"Oh her. She's just a friend. That's all." He answered.

"Does she know that?" I asked.

"Yeah. She knows. Now you do too." He replied. We went on to talk about other stuff before leaving. On my way home after picking up the twins, it still circled in my head. I'm a woman. If I say something like that on social media, there is a reason for me doing so. I should have ran away like Usain Bolt, but I didn't. I believed him.

After that night at Matches, his attitude started to change. He didn't respond to calls or text. He didn't call me or message me. Her posts continued to reveal more of a relationship than a "just friends" situation. I thought about pulling a "Waiting to Exhale Angela Bassett" move, but I decided against it. I gave him space. But it started to gnaw at me. I need to know why, as friends, he couldn't be honest. *If we are friends, you should feel comfortable with telling me who she is. What's wrong with that?* I asked on Facebook messenger.

I told you we are friends! That's it! Was his response. After that, he blocked me on social media. I started retracing my steps. What did I do? What was the problem? A small piece of my heart separated from me. I felt like I was on punishment, but I had no clue what I did.

I went back to my normal life of work and being an awesome mom. Man or not, Lola and Josiah would never suffer because of my personal issues. When my little sister Nicole came, it was the burst of love I needed. She played with her niece and nephew. We went sightseeing when we could. The real reason she was here, however, was to see Fantasia and Maxwell in concert. We went to that concert and had so much fun! Then, I went to the restroom. When I left the restroom, I saw Donovan in line waiting to get a beer. I did my best to maneuver around people so he couldn't see me. I made it back to my seat and did my best to put on a brave face. I was NOT going to let Donovan mess this night up.

Once the concert was over, he realized I was there when our eyes connected by the exit. My sister and I were walking to our car in the parking garage.

"Lalani! Lalani! Yo! Wait up!" I turned around to see Donovan and the Facebook girl walking towards us.

"What do you want me to do?" Nicole asked.

"Nothing. Just get in the car." I answered.

"Lalani! Wait up!" He screamed again. I rolled my eyes and turned around.

"Hey! How are you?" He asked.

"Excuse me? Do I know you?" I asked.

"C'mon. Don't play." He leaned for a hug and I held up my hand.

"Oh...so you know me now? And who is this?" I ask about the girl behind him.

"Hi. My name is Lalani. Nice to meet you. And you are?" I ask.

"Oh yeah. This is Latoya." He said nonchalantly.

"Just...Latoya? That's it? Not Girlfriend or 'BAE' Latoya?" I asked. Nicole tried her best to hide her snicker.

"Yes. Just Latoya. How are you?"

"I'm fine."

"Haven't heard from you in a while."

"I know."

"We should talk some time."

"Ok."

"Well...be safe getting home." He said. I stood by the car for a while with the craziest look on my face. Was I in the twilight zone? What did I just witness?

"Lani...you good?" Nicole asked.

"Yeah...Yeah. Let's go."

A couple of weeks later, Facebook revealed that Donovan and Latoya were no longer together. A couple of days after that, Donovan started calling like nothing ever happened. I tried to stay angry, but I couldn't. I allowed him back into my life and my heart. I wanted him to love me like I loved him. I wanted him in whatever way I could have him.

Chapter 5

The "Second Time Around" is not just a great song by Shalamar. It was a perfect description of my relationship with Donovan after the concert. I chalked up the first incident to miscommunication and forgave him.

Our second start to a relationship was slow. Our communication still needed some work, but our bedroom manners did not. What we shared between those sheets was magnetic. We listened to each other's bodies. We let hands move and bodies melt until we were one. It was powerful and nurturing. Ne-Yo's "Lazy Love" probably described it best.

It took a while, but we started to talk more. The more we talked, the more I felt like the relationship was growing. I was always open and honest about everything. He still chose to have his guard up. I made a point to add as much as I could to his life. I cooked and left dinner. I tried as much as possible to keep things interesting, loving, and fun. I'm sure you've probably noticed that the only person going above and beyond is me.

A few months pass and I start to hear from him less. Not as many calls. Fewer text messages. He said it was work related. His job as a marketing supervisor for a major retail company was very demanding, so I gave him space to take care of his business. Unfortunately, he was doing more with that space than I expected.

I was doing my normal scrolling through Facebook. I came across a picture Donovan was tagged in. It was him with some woman. She looked familiar, but I couldn't exactly pinpoint how until I talked to my sister. Nicole informed me that she was from back home, and she went to college with the young lady. When I asked Donovan about her, I was told to not pay attention to what is on Facebook because, and I quote, "Social media ruins relationships." (How in the hell does an app that you control ruin a relationship?) As I continued to press the issue, his irritation increased to the point where he hung up on me. That was our last conversation for a while. I swear I wanted him to smell my fist on purpose, but I honestly wanted to punch myself. Why do I allow him opportunities to lie to me? Why did I allow him to make me feel unimportant? Why did I compare myself to these women? I cried and complained with my anger, but it was in vain and pointless.

A few months later, Donovan's relationship with the woman ended. And where did he end up? In my face apologizing for his actions. In my face telling me he made the biggest mistake of his life. In my face stating he would never take our friendship for granted. Notice I said friendship. NOT relationship. And what did I do? I listened. I even consoled him. However, I didn't believe him. Each time he chose someone else over me, my heart broke a little more. I still held on to this dream of us. A dream that was slowly turning into a non-existent reality.

Chapter 6

Seven months after his failed relationship, listening and consoling turned into us communicating again. I tried to take my time this time letting my guard down. I know... I know. You are probably telling me "The hell? You better build a wall with barbed wire, cameras, and motion sensors that release missiles at trespassers!" You're not wrong for thinking this.

I let Donovan know that I moved to a city four hours away for a better paying job. He started making trips to see me every other weekend just so we could hang out. Sometimes, he would bring his daughter so she could play with my kids. Lola and Josiah knew who he was, and they actually liked him. Christmas came around, and we were in our own little world. The kids were opening gifts. Donovan and I exchanged gifts. If I'm honest, that was completely unexpected.

Usually, I'm the one buying gifts, but when he handed me a box wrapped in shiny silver paper and a red bow, my eyes widened. He was finally doing it. He was maturing.

After we exchanged gifts, he had to get back on the road to be at work the next morning. As he was getting up to leave, I asked him if we could talk.

"About what?" He asked.

"Well...I just want to say thank you. I feel like you are actually taking this relationship seriously." I responded.

"Relationship?"

"Yeah...me and you."

"Oh. Look Lani...I'm not in a space to be in a committed relationship. I... I'm still trying to figure out me."

"Oh?" I blinked really fast.

"Yeah. I mean it's cool that we've been kickin' it. And I've enjoyed it. But after dealing with a selfish and childish woman,

I kinda want to take a minute and figure out how to work on me. Does that make sense?"

I sat back on the sofa. "Yeah. I mean... Yes, it does. I guess... I'll talk to you soon?"

He started to get up. "Yeah. I'll call you once I make it home." That was the last conversation we had that year. January came, and I still heard nothing from him. I decided to start counseling to deal with some of my personal issues and self-care problems. I never really learned how to deal with my emotions. I knew how to look happy. I knew how to suppress my sadness, anger, frustration, hurt, and pain. But I was a bomb, and my timer was slowly ticking until I would explode. I had to do something, and therapy helped me to learn how to handle all emotions in a healthy manner.

I also learned the importance of boundaries. The word NO became my best friend after an assignment I had to do. I had to write a letter to people who caused me pain. Donovan received one of my letters. I mailed it with no contact information or return address. Two weeks after mailing, Donovan texted me. He told me he received my letter, and he prayed that all was well. I should have deleted the message and never responded. But...that would be "too much like right" as my grandmother would say.

He called. He had a lot to say so I let him talk. He also had an announcement: He was engaged! To whom you may ask? Just the ex-girlfriend he said he would never marry. *What kind of new-fangled bat guano is this?* I asked myself while on the phone. I refocused myself back to the conversation and congratulated him on his engagement.

"Well...I'll talk to you later..." I responded.

"Wait! Where are you going? We need to talk." He asked.

"About what?" I said with an attitude.

"About us. I... I didn't want us to fall out and not talk. I value our friendship."

"Really? Donovan you were the one who stopped talking to me. I tried to reach out to you, but you didn't answer. Were you expecting me to wait on you or beg for your friendship?"

Silence came from the other side of the phone for about 3 minutes. "I screwed up. I know. I've made the biggest mistake of my life. Can we meet and talk?"

"Do what now?"

"Can we meet and talk? In person? I think it would be better if we saw each other. I need to see you."

"D... I don't think that..."

"Lalani. Seriously. We need to talk."

Dammit! I sighed. "Ok Donovan. When?"

Chapter 7

I should have stayed home, but I went to meet Donavan. He was doing THE absolute most: all in my personal space, overly affectionate, and stupidly attentive. Every time he put his arm around me, I would kindly remind: "Uh, sir, you have a fiancé."

"But it's probably not going to work out. We just don't see eye to eye on some things." He responded.

"Time out. You are a grown ass man. Why would you propose to a woman that you are not in love with? Kinda juvenile, don't you think?"

"I know. But that's why I'm hoping to salvage our friendship. It's...it's the only thing that is keeping me sane. I want to change. I'm going to change. Just give me a chance to show you that has happened." "Ok. But you can't have your cake and fiancée' too. You need to deal with your issues and soon. You will have to make a decision. I know my value, and I will get rid of you if necessary." I answered.

Donovan and I continued to talk. He came to town to see me every once in a while. I'll admit I made the mistake of being intimate with him knowing he had a fiancée. When I prayed, I prayed for clarity. I prayed for a way to salvage what was left of our friendship (an unhealthy friendship...but still). I hoped that my prayers canceled out my wrongs. I started to realize that I may have to let him go in order to save myself.

Donovan's visits increased. He started sending more gifts and texting more often. Something had to be going on. Curiosity got the best of me, so I took a moment to troll social media. Neither Donovan nor his fiancée had posted anything pertaining to their engagement: No engagement videos, photos, sappy love posts, ring pictures, relationship status updates or photos of them together. Well, correction: SHE posted pictures from a photo shoot in Jamaica. Otherwise, nothing. Were they really engaged? Why would he lie to me about that?

About two months later, it was revealed later that the photos from Jamaica were engagement photos. She just cropped Donovan out. He still continued to prove his friendship and dedication to me through gifts and communication. I continue to interact with him, but I always prayed. I needed HIS guidance through this relationship. I also took heed of my counseling sessions as well. The greatest lesson I learned from those sessions: When you ask God to reveal things to you, you must be prepared that the answer might not be what you want.

A voice told me to check social media. I went to his fiancée's page and found a video about their upcoming wedding. I called Donovan around 10:30 PM that night.

"Hello?" He answered half asleep.

"Donovan. What is going on?" I asked.

"What are you talking about, Lalani?" He answered.

"Lalani? You never call me that. Wait. Is she there?" I asked. Donovan went silent for about 2 minutes.

"Look, Lalani, can we talk tomorrow? Please?" He asked.

"Yeah. Whatever." I hung up the phone and looked at the ceiling for most of the night wondering how in the world I got to this point. I realized that I put myself into this position, and I cannot blame Donovan for something I allowed to happen. While I wanted to be angry at him, my love for him was stronger. I calmed myself down.

I got up the next morning peacefully. I came to terms with the choices, and I was prepared to talk to Donovan calmly but honestly.

"Hi Lani." Donovan said.

"Hi. I apologize for last night." I responded calmly and quietly.

Donovan took a deep breath. "It's ok. You have the right to do so. I... I just wanted you to know that I'm marrying her. I thought about it for the longest time, and I don't want to embarrass her or myself with cancelling the wedding. Plus, she's the type that fits the image I want."

"The 'image' you want?"

"Yeah...you know... successful, light-skinned, well-dressed, no kids. If I'm honest, I never planned on picking you anyway." Each of his words squeezed my lungs until I couldn't breathe for about 10 seconds.

"Wow. Well, thank you for your complete honesty. I won't say that I am not hurt. I know you waited. You waited to tell me these words so I wouldn't leave until you were ready for me to do so. I appreciate you because I learned a lot about what I will not accept from someone in a relationship. Utmost blessings to you both." I answered. I heard something fall over.

"Your desk fell over?" I asked.

"No. I pushed it over! Why can't we be friends for each other?" He shouted.

"You chose a wife. Give her your all. I expect that of you and more. I appreciate you, and I wish you the best. Goodbye Donovan." Click.

Chapter 8

Three weeks had passed, and I was working on my happiness. During these weeks, I took the time to truly evaluate myself, Donovan, and our relationship. The fantasy I had been striving towards for so long was not my reality, but it was for a good reason. There are tons of good people in this world. However, that doesn't mean they are good for you or the purpose placed in your life. I have a big heart that causes me a lot of pain. I have learned that it is a gift that must be used with wisdom just like any other gift.

95% of my relationship with Donovan was a struggle. I struggled with seeing my value based on how he valued me. Truth is...he projected his brokenness onto me. No matter how much love I gave him, it would never be enough. Donovan's actions were always based on his present emotions. They were impulsive, and he never wanted to take responsibility for his actions. I painted Donovan to be perfect even when he showed me his true colors. I broke my own heart by looking beyond his reality at his potential.

Donovan saying that he would never choose me shattered my heart. This had been a painful journey, but I chose to learn from it. I started spending more time in prayer and reading my Bible. Scriptures state that "all things work together for our good". One day, while in prayer, God spoke these simple words to me: "You chose him. NOT me!" Well hell...there you have it. There was the undeniable truth. I chose Donovan. Donovan was not the man God selected for me.

This is why it took so much out of me in trying to keep him in my life. Donovan was everything a woman could ask for on the exterior. His interior, however, consisted of no substance. I was pouring into someone who didn't have the capacity to pour back into me. We were not equally yoked! The sad, heartbreaking truth is that I am not the only one. I am not the only one who loved the potential of someone while the reality of the individual was sucking the life out of them.

While I was healing my heart, I was also praying for forgiveness and wisdom. As I understood myself better, I also identified the things that were non-negotiables for me in a spouse. Since you all already know most of my business, why not share these with you? I want the following:

1.   A man of faith

2.   Someone faithful and honest

3.   A healthy communicator (A person who talks AND listens to understand)

4.   A person who loves me the way God intended for me to be loved

5.   A man who is aware of who he is and walks in his truth

I'm sure you are thinking Donovan is complete out of the picture, right? Eh...not quite. I was over it, but he wasn't. Ironic, huh? He texted me asking how I was doing. Then, he tells me that the wedding was called off, and he's having trouble at his job. I recommended that he reach out to his fiancée in an effort to work things out. Then, my phone started ringing.

"Hello?" I asked.

"Are you ok?" Donovan's voice asked. I couldn't help but shake my head.

"Why do you ask?"

"Why are you being short with me?" He asked.

"I'm not sure what you are expecting from me, Donovan..." I answered.

"Well...yeah but..."

"I am not your safety net, D. Don't misunderstand. I forgave you, but I will never forget what you said. People have this crazy idea that words mean nothing. They mean something. And from you... they meant everything. I appreciate the journey, but this is where I get off the ride. I pray you find what you are looking for." CLICK. I exhaled and went back to my work. Then, my phone rings... again.

"Hey," Donovan started, "Are we still friends?"

What in the hot tamales in a box was

happening! This dude is really wasting my unlimited minutes! "Donovan, you didn't value me, or my friendship. It showed in your actions. Being someone's friend is a title that is earned. You didn't see me as a friend. You saw me as a convenience. You were selfish. You were dishonest, and you used our friendship as a leverage against my loyalty. All I ever wanted was you. I wanted you to sincerely love me, but that was too much to ask, right? Each time you walked away, I found peace in your absence. I have no bad or malicious feelings towards you, but friendship is not in our dictionary. So, to answer your question... NO. We are not friends. BUT I wish you well."

"Well, can I check on you every now and then?" He asked. I dropped my head. This dude...

"I have no intentions of changing my number, D. If you do so, that's fine. If you don't, that's ok too. Thanks for the talk. Take care."

CLICK. And... Change ringer to SILENT.

Chapter 9

Six months separate myself from my last conversation with Donovan. Yes, I'm currently single, but I am living the BEST single life. I am not wavering when it comes to my non-negotiables! I have started a new business during this time and aging like fine wine. I'm not proud of all the pieces of my story, but I sure as hell am proud of myself from learning from the experiences and choosing to be a better version of myself.

If you are reading my story, please know that it is not your responsibility to heal someone else. That is an inside job. Self-healing is a choice we must all make for ourselves. If anyone makes you question your value in a relationship, remove yourself. You are powerful and purpose filled, so walk in your purpose. I know this is cliché, but it still rings true. No one is perfect. However, there is someone perfect for you. This person will also pour into you like you do for them. You are extraordinary and not mediocre. Don't worry or rush. Greatness takes time.

My name is Lalani Elizabeth Jones. This is a piece of my story. I had to struggle in order to conquer it. Whether you are male or female, Christian or not, I hope my story encourages you, strengthens you, and even comforts you. Now, let me get back to living my best life and sharing all this Black Girl Magic with the world!

Get Connected With Author Christina Louise On Social Media.

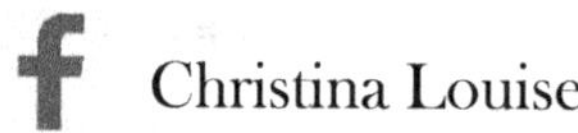
Christina Louise

Christinalouise01